PUFFIN BOOKS
Editor: Kaye Webb

MY NAUGHTY
LITTLE SISTER'S FRIENDS

When my mother said: 'Wouldn't you like to go on a visit one day?' my naughty little sister would say: 'I'm not sure.'

She said: 'I should like to sleep in a different bed with a different picture on the wall and eat different dinners, but I don't think I should like to go a long way to do it.'

So kind Mrs Cocoa next door asked her to go on a visit. She stayed next door all weekend and slept in the little bed and ate Mrs Cocoa's dinners, and it was all very strange and pleasant. When she played in Mrs Cocoa's garden she didn't even look at our house. She was really being away on a visit.

My naughty little sister had other friends as well as Mrs Cocoa. There was the guard in the train who let her sit with him in his van, and her friend Harry who went all on his own to visit her, and walked through the snow in his slippers. There was the old old aunt she gave a toy snow-storm to on her hundredth birthday, the sweep who cleaned all the lovely tempting black soot out of the chimney, and Winnie who came to tea wearing the prettiest ringlets.

More of these charming stories, ideal for bedtime reading aloud, are told in *My Naughty Little Sister, When My Naughty Little Sister was Good* and *My Naughty Little Sister and Bad Harry.*

Cover design by Shirley Hughes

My Naughty
Little Sister's Friends

DOROTHY EDWARDS

Illustrated by Una J. Place

PUFFIN BOOKS

Puffin Books, Penguin Books Ltd, Harmondsworth, Middlesex, England
Penguin Books, 625 Madison Avenue, New York, New York 10022, U.S.A.
Pengiun Books Australia Ltd, Ringwood, Victoria, Australia
Penguin Books Canada Ltd, 2801 John Street, Markham, Ontario, Canada L3R 1B4
Penguin Books (N.Z.) Ltd, 182–190 Wairau Road, Auckland 10, New Zealand

—

First published by Methuen 1962
Published in Puffin Books 1968
Reprinted 1969, 1971 (twice), 1972, 1973, 1974, 1975 (twice), 1976, 1977

—

—

Made and printed in Great Britain
by Hazell Watson & Viney Ltd,
Aylesbury, Bucks
Set in Linotype Granjon

TO BETTY FALK
WITH LOVE

Contents

The Cocoa Weekend   9

My Naughty Little Sister and the Guard   18

Bad Harry and the Milkman   26

The Very Old Birthday Party   34

The Cross Spotty Child   40

My Naughty Little Sister and the Sweep   48

My Naughty Little Sister is Very Sorry   56

What a Jealous Child!   66

The Smart Girl   76

My Naughty Little Sister is a Curly Girl   85

The Cocoa Weekend

WHEN I was a little girl I sometimes went to stay with my godmother-aunt in the country, for the week-end.

My mother would pack a little case for me, and then my godmother would come to spend a day with us and take me back with her.

My little sister was always very interested when she saw Mother packing my case, and she would remember things to go in it, and go and fetch them *without being asked*.

She used to ask me questions and questions about going visiting, and when I had told her everything she used to ask me all over again because she liked hearing it so much.

I told her about the nice little blue bed that I slept in at my godmother's and the picture of the big dog and the little dog on the bedroom wall. I told her and told her about them.

Then she wanted to hear about the things we had to eat and the things I did. I told her about all the tiny little baby-looking cakes that my godmother made, and about my godmother's piano, and how she let me play little made-up tunes on it if I wanted to.

And she would say: 'Tell me again about the piano,' my little sister would say: 'Tell me again. I like about the piano.'

So I would tell her about the piano all over again, and then I would pretend to play tunes on the table, and my sister would pretend to play tunes on the table too, and we would laugh and laugh.

But, when my mother said: 'Wouldn't you like to go on a visit one day?' my little sister would say: 'I'm not sure.'

My little sister told her friend Mrs Cocoa all about my goings away, and Mrs Cocoa was surprised to find how much my little sister knew about it, and *she* said: 'Wouldn't you like to go on a visit one day?' as well.

When Mrs Cocoa said this, my sister said: 'I don't think I should mind the visit but I shouldn't like the long-way-away.'

My little sister said: 'I should like to sleep in a different bed with a different picture on the wall and eat different dinners and play the piano, but I don't think I should like to go a long way to do it.'

You see my godmother-aunt did live quite a long way from our house, and my little sister was rather frightened to think what a long way it was.

Now kind Mrs Cocoa thought about what my little sister had said, and the next time she heard that I was going to stay with my godmother-aunt, she said to my little sister: 'How would you like to go away for a weekend, too? How would you like to come and stay with me?'

Mrs Cocoa said: 'You can sleep in my little spare bedroom and eat all your dinners and things with Mr Cocoa and me, and you won't be a long-way-away, will you?'

Wasn't that a lovely idea for clever Mrs Cocoa to have had? Mrs Cocoa lived next door to us, and my little sister knew her house very well, but she had never slept there and had all her dinners and things there, so it would be a real visit, wouldn't it?

My sister was very pleased. It was just what she wanted : a real visit that was not far away, so she said at once : 'Please, Mrs Cocoa, I should like that.'

So when my mother packed my case she packed one for my naughty little sister as well, and my little sister helped her to fetch things for both the cases.

When my godmother-aunt was ready to go, and I put my best hat and coat on, my sister said she must put *her* best hat and coat on too because she was going visiting just like her big sister.

Now you know there was a little gate that Mr Cocoa had made in the fence between his garden and ours, especially for my little sister so that she could come in to see Mrs Cocoa when she wanted to. It was a dear little gate and my little sister was always using it, but because she was going to visit Mrs Cocoa, she said she didn't want to go through her gate, she wanted to go through Mrs Cocoa's *front door*.

'I'm not Mrs Cocoa's next-door girl,' she said : 'I'm a visitor.'

So my father carried the case for her, and my little sister went down our front garden and through our front gate and through Mrs Cocoa's front gate and *up* her front garden and Father lifted her up so that she could knock on Mrs Cocoa's knocker.

My little sister knocked very hard and called out: 'Here I am, Mrs Cocoa; I've come to visit you!' And

Mrs Cocoa opened the door, and said: 'Well, I *am* pleased to see you, come in do. You're just in time for tea.'

'Come in, my dear,' Mrs Cocoa said, and Mr Cocoa came out into the hall and said: 'I'll take your luggage, ma'am,' just as if he hardly knew my sister at all! Wasn't that nice?

My little sister said: 'Thank you, Mr Jones.' Not Mr Cocoa. She said: 'Thank you, *Mr Jones*,' in a visitor-way.

Then she kissed our father 'good-bye' and Father

said: 'Have a good time, old lady' and then she was really on a visit by herself.

Mrs Cocoa gave my sister a very beautiful tea with all her best moss-rose tea-set on the table too, and that was exciting because although my sister had known Mrs Cocoa a long time she had never seen the moss-rose tea-set used before.

Then Mrs Cocoa took my sister upstairs to show her

where she was going to sleep, and that was exciting too, because Mrs Cocoa had found a bed-cover with flowers and dragons and gold curly things needleworked all over it that my little sister had never seen before and this was on the little bed she was to sleep in.

There was a new picture on the wall too. Mrs Cocoa had told Mr Cocoa about the picture at my godmother-aunt's house, and kind Mr Cocoa had found a picture in a book and put it in a frame specially for the visit. It was a picture of a singing lady lying in some water with flowers floating on it. Mr Cocoa said he liked the picture because the flowers and bushes and things in it looked so real.

My little sister liked the picture too. She said she liked it because the naughty lady hadn't taken her dress off, and she was wet as wet. She liked to have a picture of a naughty wet lady to look at, she said.

Weren't the Cocoas kind to think of all these nice surprises? Mr Cocoa said : 'We haven't got a piano, but I've got something else here that ought to keep you out of mischief.'

And do you know what he had? It was a musical-box! It was a little brown box with a glass window in the top, and at the side of the box there was a key. When you turned the key a little shiny thing with holes in it went round and round – you could see it through the glass window, and a pretty little tune came out of the box that Mr Cocoa said was called 'The Bluebells of Scotland'.

It you want to know what it sounded like perhaps you can ask someone to hum it for you.

Mr Cocoa showed my sister how to wind the musical-box and then he said she could play it whenever she liked. And she did play it – lots and lots of times while she was visiting.

My sister stayed with the dear Cocoa Joneses all that weekend and had a lovely time with them. She slept in the little bed and ate Mrs Cocoa's dinners and things and played the musical-box and went for walks with Mr Cocoa while Mrs Cocoa had a rest, and it was all very strange and pleasant.

But, do you know, my little sister NEVER ONCE CAME BACK HOME. She never even knocked on the wall to our mother! Not once. Mother said she saw my little sister playing in Mrs Cocoa's garden, and she watched her going off for walks, but my little sister didn't even look at our house!

She was really being away on a visit.

When the weekend was over, Mrs Cocoa packed her case for her, and Mr Cocoa took her home by the front door to show that she had been away.

When my little sister saw me again, she didn't ask about *my* visit – oh no! She told me instead all about her visit to the Cocoas. She told me about the dragon

16

and flower bed-cover and the naughty lady picture, and she said: 'There wasn't a piano, but I played another thing.'

My little sister couldn't remember the name of the musical-box though, so she said: 'I played a la-la box', and she la-la'd all the 'Bluebells of Scotland' tune for me without making one mistake. Wasn't she clever?

My Naughty Little Sister
and the Guard

Do you like trains?

When I was a little girl I didn't like trains at all; but my little sister did. I thought that trains were horrid and noisy and puffy and steamy but my little sister said they were lovely things, and when she saw one she waved and waved and shouted and shouted to it.

Well now, one day a kind aunt wrote to our mother to ask if my little sister would like to go and stay for a weekend. All by herself.

Not with my father or mother, or even with me, but all by herself like a grown-up lady!

My mother said: 'I don't think she's old enough,' and my father said: 'I don't think she's good enough,' and I said: 'She'll be too frightened.' Because, if you remember, she *had* been frightened about visiting people.

But my little sister said: 'I should like to go and stay for a weekend all by myself. I *am* an old enough girl, and I am not a frightened girl any more. I want to go!'

My mother didn't say anything and my father didn't

say anything and I didn't say anything, and my little sister knew why that was, because she said : 'I'm not a good girl now, but I will be good as gold if you will let me go.'

So my father and mother said they thought she might go if she *was* as good as gold. So my little sister was good. She was quiet and tidy and whispery all the week and when the weekend came she *did* go away. All on her own.

This is the exciting thing that happened to her.

Our kind aunt lived quite a long way away, and my little sister had to go on a train *all by herself*.

Wasn't that exciting? All by herself. She had a little brown case with her nightdress inside, and her slippers and her dressing-gown and her best dress for Sunday and all the things she had taken to dear Mrs Cocoa's. My little sister carried Rosy-Primrose under her arm, but of course Mother carried the case to the station for her.

'Auntie will meet you at the other end,' Mother said. 'So she will carry it to her house for you.'

'I hope Auntie won't forget to look for me,' said my little sister, 'because I don't think I could open a train door all by myself.'

'That's all right,' our mother told her. 'I'm going to ask the guard to keep an eye on you.'

My little sister was going to say 'What guard?' and

ask questions and questions, but she knew that Mother was in a hurry to get the ticket. When she got to the station she was very excited. She *wanted* to fidget and climb on all the parcels and run along the platform and peep at the man who puts the parcels on the weighing machine. But she didn't. She remembered about being good as gold. Wasn't she sensible?

When the train came in, she didn't rush about or fuss, she walked nicely down the platform beside Mother to where the guard was standing, and when Mother stopped to speak to the guard my little sister didn't talk at all. She just stared at the guard because he was such a big beautiful man.

The guard had a big red beautiful face and a big fluffy black moustache and a golden glittery band on his cap and a silver glittery whistle round his neck and two beautiful flags – a red one and a green one under his arm. He gave my mother and my little sister a most pleasant smile.

'I am going to put this little girl in the end carriage, Guard,' our mother said, 'and I wonder if you would be kind enough to look after her ticket for her, and see that she gets off at the right station?'

The guard smiled very kindly then at my little sister. 'She is a very little girl,' he said. 'Is she a good child? If she is, she can come in the guard's van with me for the journey.'

My little sister thought she had better say something, because she thought how nice it would be to travel in a real guard's van with a real guard, almost as nice as travelling with the engine-driver and not nearly so hot and coaly. She said : 'I am not always a good child. But I am being very good *this week*.'

So the guard said: 'That's good enough for me. In you go then,' and my sister climbed up into the guard's van.

He said: 'Sit on my little seat in the corner there.' And although it was rather a high little seat my little sister managed to climb on to it while the guard put her little case into the van, and picked up some parcels from the platform and put them in too.

Then the guard took his green flag, and blew his whistle, and Mother called out: 'Good-bye, give my love to Auntie,' and the train started to move. The guard jumped in quickly and shut the door. And they were off!

What a very nice man the guard was! He talked all the time to my little sister. He showed her a lantern that made red and green lights, and let her look at some sheets of paper with lines and printing on them that he said he had to write on every day. He lent my sister a pencil and let her scribble on the back of one of his pieces of paper, but it was very difficult because the train was so bumpy, so he gave her an apple to eat instead.

Each time the train stopped at a station the guard jumped down and took in parcels and sacks and put other parcels and sacks on to the platform. Sometimes there were railway porters waiting for the van, with trucks full of luggage, and they stared at my sister and asked the guard who she was. 'Oh, she's my new Mate,' the guard said, and my little sister felt proud as proud.

At one station the guard took in a big basket full of chickens, all looking out in a very pecky way. But the guard told my sister they wouldn't really hurt anyone. 'I often bring chickens,' he said, 'and ducks and dogs and cats.'

He said that one day he took a very growly dog that grumbled all the time. 'I was glad to see the back of him,' the guard said.

Then he said : 'Yes, I've looked after a lot of animals since I've been on the Line, but you are the first little girl.'

My little sister liked to think that she was the first little girl to travel with the guard, and she said : 'If you have any other little girls to mind you'll be able to tell them about me.' And the guard said that he certainly would.

At last they came to the station that was near our aunt's house, and there was Auntie herself and two of our cousins as well, all waiting for her, and all so happy to see my little sister.

'There's Auntie!' my sister said, and she jumped up and down with excitement as the guard began to open the door.

But she remembered to be a polite child even though she was excited, and before she went off she shook hands

with the guard and said: 'Thank you for having me' –
just like a party – 'thank you for having me.'

And the guard said: 'It has been a real pleasure,' and
when the train moved off again, he stayed by his window so as to wave to my little sister and she waved to
him. How our cousins stared to see a guard waving
from his guard's van window at my little sister.

So my little sister stayed with our auntie for a weekend and she wasn't naughty once. On Monday when
she came back home Auntie came with her, because
she wanted to come up for the day to see our mother, so

my sister didn't travel in the guard's van that time; but she remembered all about it, and when she and Bad Harry played trains in the garden she said: 'I must be the guard because I know all about it.'

And she did, didn't she?

Bad Harry and the Milkman

LONG ago, when my sister was a naughty little girl and not a grown-up lady, she had a friend called Harry. Harry was a naughty boy, so he and my sister were very good friends.

Harry and my sister were very noisy when they played together. If they saw anything funny they would laugh and laugh and roll about on the ground, and they always laughed at the same time at the same thing.

And when my sister was cross, Harry was cross, and when she was stubborn he was stubborn too, and when she said: '*I* want that!' about something, Harry always said: 'You can't have it, because *I* want it.'

My sister would shout 'Give it to me at once!' and Harry would shout 'No'.

Then my sister would jump up and down and say: 'Bad Harry' over and over again. 'Bad, bad, Harry!'

Then she would pull his hair, and he would pull her hair and they would hit each other in a very unkind way, until our mother came out and grumbled at them. Then they would stop fighting.

But they went on being friends just the same.

But when Harry came to our house or she went to Harry's house, she had to say 'Bad Harry' so many times that we called him Bad Harry in the end, and he really was, bad as bad. Oh dear.

They were cross good friends, weren't they?

Well now, when my sister and Harry were very small, they didn't come visiting each other on their own. Our mother took my sister to Harry's house, and Harry's mother brought him round to us, and as our mothers were busy women they couldn't always be walking round to each other's houses, so there were some days when Harry and my sister couldn't see each other and they didn't like that at all.

One day, when it was cold and snowy, Harry's poor mother wasn't a very well lady, and she couldn't go out, so Harry had to stop at home and not see my sister, and he didn't like that.

Harry stood and looked out of the window, and saw the snow coming down, and everything looked very white and pretty, and he thought of all the lovely games he could have in the snow with my sister.

He thought of making snowballs and throwing them at her, as he'd seen the big boys making snowballs and throwing them at their friends, and he thought of them making a funny old snow-man with a pipe like a picture in one of his books. He thought of all sorts of nice games in the snow.

Then he got very cross and miserable in case the snow should melt before he could play with my sister again.

Then Harry had a bad idea (not a good idea – a *bad* one). He thought he would put on his coat and hat and go and visit my sister all on his own.

What a very bad Harry.

The next-door lady who had come in to make Harry's breakfast had gone home for a little while, and his mother was fast asleep in bed upstairs, so there was no one to ask.

Bad Harry went and fetched his coat and put it on. He wasn't good about buttons then, so he left it undone.

He found his woolly cap and he put that on. He forgot his gloves, and his leggings and his shoes. He *was in such a hurry*.

He opened the front door, and off he went in his bunny-slippers down the path and out into the snow. He *was* excited; he hurried to get to our house to play with my sister.

The snow fell and fell. It was swirly and curly and cold and it blew into Harry's face, and it crunched under his bunny-slippers, and he thought it was very exciting.

Now all the people who lived in Harry's road had very kindly swept the snow from the pavements in front of their houses so it was quite easy for Harry to get

along, but when he turned the first corner, he came to a road where the people hadn't been so kind and thoughtful about clearing the pavements, and soon his little bunny-slippers were quite covered up when he walked.

And his feet got wet and cold.

The wind was blowing down that street too, and it threw the snow into Harry's face in a very unkind way, and Harry suddenly found that his fingers were cold too.

His feet were cold and his fingers were cold, and he

hadn't done his coat up so he was all cold. Cold as cold.

And because he was only a little boy then, Harry did a silly little boy thing. He stood quite still. He opened his mouth and he started to cry and cry.

Now, we had a very nice milkman who came to our house. He was a great friend of my little sister's. This milkman had an old white horse and a jingly cart and when he came down the road he would call out 'M-I-L-K-O! M-I-L-K-O!'

Like that, and when he came to the door he would sing: 'Milk for the babies, cream for the ladies! M-I-L-K-O!' He was a nice milkman.

He was *just* the person to come along with his white horse and jingly cart and find poor Bad Harry crying because he was cold.

Down the road he came, jingle jingle rather slowly because of the snow on the road, and his old white horse walking carefully, carefully. And he saw Harry.

He saw cold Harry crying so he said 'Wo-a there' to his old white horse, and the milk-cart stopped and he got down and said: 'Why, you're the little chap who plays with young Saucy down the next street.'

When the milkman said 'young Saucy down the next street' he meant my sister, because he always called her that (although it wasn't her name of course).

When the nice milkman saw how cold poor Harry was, and how miserable he was, he put him into his milk-cart and wrapped him up in a rug that was on the seat, and because he didn't know where Harry lived, he took him round to our house, which wasn't very far away – only round the next corner after all!

Now my sister was standing by *our* kitchen window being as cross as cross, and wanting to play in the snow with Harry, when she saw the milkman stopping at the gate.

She was very surprised when she saw him lift a bundle in a rug out of his cart and carry it up our path, so she ran to the door with Mother to see what it was all about.

When they opened the door they heard Harry bellowing and crying because he was so cold, and Mother thanked the milkman for bringing him and took him in quickly to warm by our fire.

Poor Harry! Mother rubbed and rubbed him and gave him hot milk and made him sit with his feet in a bowl of hot water, until he stopped crying and told her that he had come round *all on his own*.

My sister *did* open her eyes when she heard this! On his own!

Mother told Harry that he had been very *naughty*. She said his mother might be very, very worried, and she sent me round at once to tell Harry's next-door lady where he was.

My sister stared hard at Harry when our mother told

31

him he had been naughty and that his mother would be worried. When our mother scolded Harry he began to cry again, and this time my naughty little sister cried as well.

And they made so much noise that Mother forgave Harry and fetched him a biscuit, and he stopped crying.

My sister stopped crying too and Mother gave her a biscuit, and they sat quiet as quiet until I came back with Harry's shoes and some dry socks and leggings for him to put on, so that I could take him home again.

I told him that his next-door lady had said that his mother was still asleep and if we hurried we could get back before the poor not-well lady woke up.

So Harry hurried back with me and he was home again before his mother could wake up and worry.

Next day it was even more cold, and when the milk-man came my sister saw that he had put some funny little red-woollen bag things on his horse's ears.

She said: 'Why has your horse got those funny bag-things, milkman?'

And the nice milkman laughed and said: 'In case we have to pick up that bad friend of yours again. He yelled so much he made my horse's ears twitch. He might give her earache next time.'

And my sister looked very good, and she said in a very quiet voice: 'I am afraid Harry is a Bad Boy.'

The Very Old Birthday Party

LONG ago, when my sister was a naughty little girl, we had a very old, old great-Auntie who lived in a big house with lots of other very old ladies and gentlemen.

Our mother used to go and visit this old Auntie sometimes and she used to tell us all about her. Then, one day our mother said: 'How would you like to come with me to visit Dear Old Auntie?'

Our mother said: 'She is going to have a birthday party next week, and I think it would be very nice if you little girls could come to it. You see it is a very special party because old Auntie will be one hundred years old.'

One hundred years! That is very, very old. You ask some big person to tell you how old that means.

Well, *I* knew how old a hundred years was, so I said: 'Good gracious, what an old lady!'

My sister didn't know how old it was then because she was so little, but she said: 'good gracious' too, because I had.

'She is a very sweet little old lady,' our mother told us. 'Everyone likes her. The lady who looks after all the old ladies and gentlemen says that Dear Old Auntie is the *pride* of the Home.'

Wasn't that a nice thing for our old Auntie to be? The pride of the Home. We thought it was anyway, and we were very pleased to think that we were going to visit such a dear old lady on her one hundredth birthday.

Well now, when the birthday came, we were both very excited. We wore our best Sunday dresses and looked very smart girls.

Our mother had told us that we might take some money from our money-boxes to buy a present for our Dear Old Auntie in the Woolworths shop. Our mother let us choose our own presents too. I bought our Dear Old Auntie a nice little white handkerchief with blue flowers on the corner. It took me a long time to think what to buy.

But my little sister didn't think at all. She knew just what she wanted. She said: 'I am going to buy one of those glassy-looking things with the little houses inside that make it snow when you shake them.'

My little sister had been to the Woolworths shop with Mrs Cocoa, so she knew all about these glassy things.

Do you know about them? They are very pretty.

I thought it was a silly thing to give to such a very old lady, but my naughty little sister said: 'It isn't silly. I would like one of those glassy things for *my* birthday!'

And she said she wouldn't buy anything else, so our mother took her along to the toy-counter and let her pay for one of the glassy things with her own money.

So, when we went to visit the Birthday Old Lady we had some nice presents for her. I had the handkerchief and my sister had the glassy thing with the snow inside it, and Mother had a box of sweeties from my father, and a nice woollen shawl that Mrs Cocoa Jones had kindly knitted from some wool that Mother had bought.

Wasn't she a lucky old lady?

My sister and I had never been to an old people's Home before, so we were very quiet and staring when we got there.

There were so many old people. Dear old ladies and dear old gentlemen all with white hair and smiling faces, and they all talked to us and waved to us and shook hands with us in a very friendly way.

And we smiled too. My sister smiled *and* smiled.

The lady who looked after the old people was called Miss Simmons and she was very kind.

'We are all very glad to see such young people,' she said to my sister. 'Do you know I don't think we've ever had anyone quite as young as you before?'

My sister was very pleased to think that she was the first very young visitor, and she did something that she sometimes did to Mr and Mrs Cocoa Jones. *She blew kisses*. She was being nice.

Our dear old great-Auntie was sitting by the fire in a big chair, and when Miss Simmons took us over to meet her, she was very pleased to see us.

What a very little old wrinkly pretty lady our old Auntie was! She had a tiny soft little voice and twinkly little eyes and she took a great fancy to my naughty sister at once. She asked her to sit next to her. Wasn't that a nice thing for my sister to be asked to do?

The old Auntie was very pleased with her presents. She put the shawl on straight away, and she put my handkerchief into her sleeve straight away too. But when she saw what my sister had brought she clapped her hands together in a funny old-lady way and she said: 'Well-well-well. What a lovely treat! I haven't seen one of these since I was a little girl. I saw one in another little girl's house and I always wanted one. Now I've got one at last.'

And the dear old lady shook up the glassy thing and made the snow fall on to the little house, and then she shook it again and made the snow fall again. She did it so many times that we knew how very pleased she was.

'Just fancy,' she said, 'I wanted one when I was a little girl like you, and I've got one today on my hundredth birthday.'

Miss Simmons said : 'I see you have a box of sweeties too. But I don't think you had better eat them yet. We have a birthday cake with one hundred candles for you to cut and a very nice birthday tea. It would be a pity to eat sweeties and spoil your appetite.'

Now my sister had heard Mother say that sort of

thing to her but she was surprised to think that people had to say such things to old ladies, and she stared rather hard at her dear old Auntie.

And what do you think? When kind Miss Simmons went off to see about the birthday tea, old Auntie opened her box of sweeties, and gave one to me and one to my sister and then she ate one herself!

And she laughed and my sister laughed.

When Miss Simmons came back and saw what old Auntie had done she shook her finger at her. 'You are a very naughty old lady,' Miss Simmons said.

Then Miss Simmons looked at the hundred-years-old lady, and my bad little sister, both laughing together and she said: 'Goodness me, you can see you are relations. *You both look alike!*'

And do you know, when I looked, and Mother looked, at the naughty old lady and my naughty little sister, we saw that they did!

The Cross Spotty Child

ONE day, a long time ago, my naughty little sister wasn't at all a well girl. She was all burny and tickly and tired and sad and spotty and when our nice doctor came to see her he said : 'You've got measles, old lady.'

'You've got measles,' that nice doctor said, 'and you will have to stay in bed for a few days.'

When my sister heard that she had measles she began to cry: 'I don't want measles. Nasty measles,' and made herself burnier and ticklier and sadder than ever.

Have you had measles? Have you? If you have you will remember how nasty it is. I am sure that if you did have measles at any time you would be a very good child. You wouldn't fuss and fuss. But my sister did, I'm sorry to say.

She fidgeted and fidgeted and fussed and cried and had to be read to all the time, and wouldn't drink her orange-juice and lost her hanky in the bed until our mother said: 'Oh dear, I don't want you to have measles, I'm sure.'

She *was* a cross spotty child.

When our mother had to go out to do her shopping,

kind Mrs Cocoa Jones came in to sit with my sister.
Mrs Cocoa brought her knitting with her, and sat by
my sister's bed and knitted and knitted. Mrs Cocoa was
a kind lady and when my little sister moaned and
grumbled she said: 'There, there, duckie,' in a very
kind way.

My little sister didn't like Mrs Cocoa saying 'There,
there, duckie' to her, because she was feeling so cross
herself, so she pulled the sheet over her face and said:
'Go away, Mrs Cocoa.'

But Mrs Cocoa didn't go away, she just went on
knitting and knitting until my naughty little sister
pulled the sheet down from her face to see what Mrs
Cocoa could be doing and whether she had made her
cross.

But kind Mrs Cocoa wasn't cross – she was just sorry
to see my poor spotty sister, and when she saw my sister
looking at her, she said: 'Now, I was just thinking. I
believe I have the very thing to cheer you up.'

My sister was surprised when Mrs Cocoa said this
instead of being cross with her for saying 'Go away' so
she listened hard and forgot to be miserable.

'When I was a little girl,' Mrs Cocoa said, 'my
granny didn't like to see poor not-well children looking
miserable so she made a get-better box that she used to
lend to all her grandchildren when they were ill.'

Mrs Cocoa said: 'My granny kept this box on top of

her dresser, and when she found anything that she thought might amuse a not-well child she would put it in her box.'

Mrs Cocoa said that it was a great treat to borrow the get-better box because although you knew some of the things that would be in it, there was always something fresh.

My little sister stopped being cross and moany while she listened to Mrs Cocoa, because she hadn't heard of a get-better box before.

She said: 'What things, Mrs Cocoa? What was in the box?'

'All kinds of things,' Mrs Cocoa said.

'Tell me! Tell me!' said my spotty little sister and she began to look cross because she wanted to know so much.

But Mrs Cocoa said: 'I won't tell you, for *you can see for yourself.*'

Mrs Cocoa said: 'I hadn't thought about it until just this very minute; but do you know, I've got my granny's very own get-better box in my house and I had forgotten all about it! It's up in an old trunk in the spare bedroom. There are a lot of heavy boxes on top of the trunk, but if you are a good girl now, I will ask Mr Cocoa to get them down for me when he comes home from work. I will get the box out of the trunk and bring it in for you to see tomorrow.'

Wasn't that a beautiful idea?

Mrs Cocoa Jones said: 'I haven't seen that box for years and years, it will be quite a treat to look in it again. I am sure it will be just the thing to lend to a cross little spotty girl with measles, don't you?'

And my naughty little sister thought it *was* just the thing indeed!

So, next morning, as soon as my sister had had some bread and milk and a spoonful of medicine, Mrs Cocoa came upstairs to see her, with her grandmother's get-better box under her arm.

There was a *smiling* spotty child waiting for her today.

It was a beautiful-looking box, because Mrs Cocoa's old grandmother had stuck beautiful pieces of wallpaper on the lid and on the sides of the box, and Mrs Cocoa said that the wallpaper on the front was some that had been in her granny's front bedroom, and that on the back had been in her parlour. The paper on the lid had come from her Aunty Kitty's sitting-room; the paper on one side had been in Mrs Cocoa's mother's kitchen, while the paper on the other side which was really lovely, with roses and green dickeybirds, had come from Mrs Cocoa's own bedroom wallpaper when she was a little girl!

My sister was so interested to hear this that she almost forgot about opening the box!

But she did open it, and she found so many things that I can only tell you about some of them.

On top of the box she found a lovely piece of shining stuff folded very tidily, and when she opened it out on her bed she saw that it was covered with round sparkly things that Mrs Cocoa said were called *spangles*. Mrs Cocoa said that it was part of a dress that a real fairy-

queen had worn in a real pantomime. She said that a
lady who had worked in a theatre had given it to her
grandmother long, long ago.

Under the sparkly stuff were boxes and boxes. Tiny
boxes with pretty pictures painted on the lids, and in

every box a nice little interesting thing. A string of tiny
beads, or a little-little dollie, or some shells. In one box
was a very little paper fan, and in another there was a
little laughing clown's face cut out of paper that Mrs
Cocoa's granny had stuck there as a surprise.

My sister was so surprised that she smiled, and Mrs
Cocoa told her that her granny had put that in to make
a not-well child be surprised and smile. She said that
she remembered smiling at that box when she was a
little girl.

Mrs Cocoa's old granny had been very clever, hadn't she?

There were picture postcards in that not-well box, and pretty stones – some sparkly and some with holes in them. There was a small hard fir cone, and pieces of coloured glass that you could hold up before your eyes and look through. There was a silver pencil with a hole in the handle that you could look through too and see a magic picture.

There was a small book with pictures in it – oh, I can't remember what else!

It amused and *amused* my sister.

She took all the things out carefully and then she put them all back carefully. She shut the lid and looked at the wallpaper outside all over again.

Then she took the things out again, and looked at them and played with them and was as interested as could be!

46

And Mrs Cocoa said:
'Well, I never! That's
just what I did myself
when I was a child!'

When my sister was
better she gave the box

back to Mrs Cocoa – just
as Mrs Cocoa had given
the box back to her
granny.

Mrs Cocoa Jones laid
all the things from the
box out in the sunshine in
her back garden to air them after the measles. She said
her grandmother always did that, and because Mrs
Cocoa's granny had done it, it made it all very specially
nice for my little sister to think about.

After that, my sister often played at making a get-
better box with a boot-box that Mother gave her, and
once she drew red chalk spots on poor Rosy-Primrose's
face so that she could have measles and the get-better
box to play with.

My Naughty Little Sister
and the Sweep

ONE morning, when I was a little girl and my naughty little sister was a girl littler than me, we went downstairs to breakfast and found everything looking very funny indeed.

The table was pushed right up against the wall, and the chairs were standing on the table and they were all covered over with a big sheet. The curtains were gone from the window, and the armchairs and the pictures and the clocks and lots of other things. All gone!

My little sister was very interested to see all this, and when she looked out of the window, she saw that the armchairs and the pictures and all the other things were piled up in our back garden. My little sister *did* stare.

Clock and pictures and armchairs in the back garden, and things covered up with sheets, no curtains! Wasn't that a strange thing to find? My little sister said: 'We have got a funny home today.'

Then my mother told us that the chimney-sweep was coming to clean the chimney and that she had had to get the room ready for him. My naughty little sister was very excited because she had never seen a sweep, and she jumped and said 'Sweep' and jumped and said 'Sweep' again and again because she was so excited. Then she said: 'Won't we have any breakfast?'

'Won't we have any breakfast?' said my hungry little sister, because the chairs were standing on the table. And Mother said: 'As it is a lovely sunny morning you are going to have a picnic breakfast in the garden.'

Then my little sister was very pleased indeed because she had never had a picnic breakfast before.

She said: 'What shall we eat?' and my mother told her, 'Well, as it is a special picnic breakfast, I have made you some egg sandwiches.' Wasn't that nice? Sandwiches for breakfast! There was milk too, and bananas. My sister *did* like it!

We sat on the back doorstep and ate and ate and drank and drank because it was so nice to be eating our breakfast in the open air.

Then, just as my little sister finished her very last bite of banana, a big man with a black-dirty face came in the back gate and Mother said: 'Here is the sweep at last.'

Well, *you* know all about sweeps, but my little sister didn't, and she was so interested that my mother said she could watch the sweep so long as she didn't meddle in any way. My sister said she would be very good, so

my mother found her one of my overalls, and tied a hanky round her head to keep her hair clean, and said: 'Now you can go and watch the sweep.'

My little sister watched the sweep man push the brush up the chimney and she watched when he screwed a cane on to the brush and a cane on to that cane, and a cane on to that cane, all the time pushing the brush up and up the chimney, and she stayed as good as good. She was very quiet. *She didn't say a thing.*

She was so mousy-quiet that the black sweep man said: 'You are quiet, missy, haven't you got a tongue?'

My sister was very surprised when the sweep asked if she had got a tongue, so she stuck her tongue out quickly to show that she had got one, and he said: 'Fancy that now!'

Then my little sister laughed and the sweep laughed and she wasn't quiet any more. She talked and talked until he had finished his work.

Then my sister asked the sweep what he was going to do with all the soot he had collected and he said: 'I shall leave it for your father to use in his garden. It's good for frightening off the tiddy little slugs.'

So, when the sweep man went away he left a little pile of soot in the garden for our father. My sister was sorry when he went away, and she asked my mother lots of questions. She wanted to know so many things

that Mother said : 'If I answer you now I'll never get the place straight, so just you run off and play like a good girl, and I will tell you all about soot and chimney-sweeps later on.'

So my sister went off, and Mother cleaned up the room and brought in the chairs and hung up curtains and did all the other tidying up things and all the time my sister was very quiet.

There had been lots of things my sister had wanted to know very badly. One thing she had wanted to know was if there was soot in *all* the chimneys. She wondered if there was any soot in her own bedroom chimney.

She went upstairs and looked up her chimney but she couldn't see because it was too dark up there.

It was very dark and my sister probably wouldn't

have bothered any more about it, only she happened to remember that there was a long cane on the landing with a feather duster on the top, that Mother used for getting the cobwebs from the top of the stairs.

Yes, I thought you would guess. The cane was very bendy and it wasn't difficult for a little girl to push it up the chimney.

Have you ever done anything so very silly as this? If you have you will know how dirty soot is. It's much dirtier than mud even.

My silly sister pushed the feather duster up her bedroom chimney and a lot of soot fell down into the fireplace. It was such a lot of soot and it looked so dirty that my little sister got frightened and wished that she hadn't done such an awful thing.

She couldn't help thinking that Mother would be very cross when she saw it.

So she thought she had better *hide it*.

You will never guess where that silly child tried to hide the soot. IN HER BED.

Yes, in her own nice clean little comfortable bed.

I'm glad to think that you wouldn't be so silly.

My sister made such a mess carrying the soot across the room and touching things with her sooty fingers and treading on the floor with sooty feet that she didn't know what to do.

She saw how messy her bedroom was and she was

53

very, very sorry; she was **so sorry** that she ran right
downstairs to the garden where Mother was shaking
the mats and she flung her little sooty arms round
Mother's skirt, and pushed her little sooty face into
Mother's apron, and she said: 'Oh, I have been a bad
girl. I have been a bad girl. Scold me a lot. Scold me a
lot.' And then she cried and cried and cried and cried
and *cried*.

And she was so sorry and so ashamed that Mother
forgave her even though it made her a lot of extra work
on a very busy day.

My little sister was so sorry that she fetched things
and carried things and told Mother when the sheets
were dry and helped to lay the table for dinner and be-

haved like the best child in England, so that our father said it was almost worth having her behave so badly when she could show afterwards what a good girl she really was.

Our father was a very funny man.

My Naughty Little Sister
is Very Sorry

A LONG time ago, when I was a little girl with a naughty little sister, a cross lady lived in our road. This cross lady was called Mrs Lock and she didn't like children.

Mrs Lock didn't like children at all, and if she saw a boy or girl stopping by her front gate she would tap on her window to them and say: 'Don't hang about here' in a very grumbling voice.

Wasn't that a cross thing to do? I will tell you why Mrs Lock was so cross. It was because she had a very beautiful garden outside her front door and once some boys had been playing football in the roadway, and the ball had bounced into her garden and broken down a beautiful rose-tree.

So when Mrs Lock saw children by her gate she thought they were going to start playing with footballs and damage her garden, and she always sent them away. Sometimes she came right out of the house and down to the gate and said: 'Go and play in the park – the roadway is no place for games,' and she would look

so fierce and cross that the children would hurry away
at once.

There was another reason too, why Mrs Lock was
so cross. You see, she had a beautiful smoky-looking
cat, and one day a nasty child had thrown a stone at the
cat and hurt his poor leg, so if Mrs Lock saw a boy or

girl stroking her smoky-looking cat, she would say:
'Don't you meddle with that cat, now!'

What a cross lady she was! But I suppose you
couldn't really blame her. It isn't nice to have your rose-
trees broken, and it's very, very bad to have your poor
cat injured, isn't it?

Well now: one bright sunshiny morning, my

naughty little sister went out for a little walk down the road all by herself. It was only a very small walk, just as far as the lamp-post at the corner of the road and back again, but my little sister was pretending that it was a very long walk; she was pretending that she was a shopping lady, stopping at all the hedges and gate-ways and saying that they were shops.

My little sister had a lovely game, all by herself, being a shopping-lady. It was a very nice day, and she had a little cane shopping-basket just like our mother's and a little old purse full of beads for pennies.

First my little sister stopped at a hedge and said: 'I'll have a nice cabbage today, please.' Then she picked a leaf and pretended that it was a cabbage, and put it carefully into her basket. She took two beads out of her purse and left them under the hedge to pay for it.

She went on until she came to a wall; there were two

little round stones by the wall, so she pretended that they were eggs and bought them too.

Then she found a piece of red flower-pot which made nice meat for her pretend dinner. She had a lovely game.

Just as she arrived at Mrs Lock's gate, the big smoky-looking cat jumped up on to it and began to purr and purr and as he purred his big feathery tail went all curly and twisty and he looked very beautiful. My sister stopped to look at him.

When the big smoky-looking cat saw my sister looking at him, he opened his mouth and showed her all his sharp little teeth, then he stretched out his curly pink tongue and began to lick one of his legs. He licked and licked.

My little sister was very pleased to see such a nice cat and she stood tippy-toed and touched him. When she did this he stopped licking and began to purr again. He was nice and warm and furry, so she stroked him, very gently towards his tail because Mother had told us that pussies didn't like being stroked the other way. 'Dear pussy. Nice animal,' she said to him.

Now, as my sister was such a little girl Mrs Lock didn't see her standing by the gate, so she didn't say 'go away' to her, and my sister had a long talk with the smoky-looking cat.

She told him that she was a shopping-lady. 'I have

bought lots of things,' she said. 'I can't think of anything else.'

When she said this, the cat got up suddenly and jumped right off the gate back into Mrs Lock's garden, and as he jumped the gate opened wide. 'Meeow,' he said. 'Meeow' – like that.

My bad little sister looked through the gate and she saw the smoky cat going up the path. She saw all the pretty tulip flowers and the wallflowers growing on each side, and do you know what she said?

She said: 'That was very kind of you, Pussy. Now I can buy a nice cup to drink my milk out of.'

And she walked into Mrs Lock's garden. Mrs Lock's

tulip flowers were all different colours: red, yellow, pink, and white. You know that tulip flowers look rather like cups, don't you?

Yes. You know.

I'll have a yellow cup, please,' my bad sister said. 'Here's the money, Pussy.'

And she picked a yellow tulip head and put it in her basket.

The smoky-looking cat walked round and round her legs, and his long tickly tail waved and waved and he said: 'Purr' to my little sister who was pretending to be a shopping-lady.

And Mrs Lock saw her from her front window.

Mrs Lock *was* cross. She tapped hard on her window glass and my naughty little sister saw her. Then she remembered that she wasn't really a shopping-lady, she remembered that she was a little girl. She remembered that it was naughty to pick flowers that didn't belong to you.

Of course you know what she did? Yes. She ran away, through the gate and down the road to our house, while Mrs Lock tapped and tapped and the smoky cat stood still in surprise.

My little sister ran straight indoors and straight upstairs and hid herself under the bed.

Mrs Lock came down the road after her, and when she saw my little sister run into the house, she came and knocked at our door, and told our mother all about my little sister's bad behaviour.

My mother was very sorry to hear that my sister had picked one of Mrs Lock's tulips, and when Mrs Lock had gone, our mother went upstairs and peeped under the bed. You see, she knew *just* where her naughty little girl would be.

'Come out,' Mother said in a kind voice, because she knew my little sister was ashamed of herself, and my little sister came out very slowly, and stood by the side of the bed and looked very sad; but Mother was so nice that my sister told her all about the pretending game

and the pussy cat, and Mother explained to her that you have to think even when you're pretending hard, and not do naughty things by mistake.

Then she told my sister all about why Mrs Lock was cross. About her rose-tree and the nasty thing that had happened to the smoky-looking cat. And my sister was very, very sorry.

When Mother went downstairs again my sister had a good idea. She went to her toy-box and she found the beautiful card that our granny had sent her for her birthday. It had a pretty picture of a pussy cat and a bunch of roses on it. It was the nicest card my sister had ever had, but she thought she would give it to Mrs Lock to show that she was sorry.

She didn't say a word to anyone. She went out very quietly down the road to Mrs Lock's gate.

When she got there, my little sister went inside the gate and up the path. The smoky-looking cat came round the side of the house to meet her, but she didn't stop to stroke him. No. She went up to Mrs Lock's front door, and rattled the letter box, then she pushed the postcard inside. She put her mouth close to the letter box and shouted : 'I am sorry I took your flower, Mrs Lock. I am very-very sorry. I have brought you my best postcard for a present.' And then she ran away again. Only this time Mrs Lock didn't tap the glass.

The very next time my little sister went by Mrs

Lock's gate there was Mrs Lock herself, pulling weeds out of her pathway, and there was the smoky-looking cat sitting on a gatepost. When the cat saw my little sister he jumped down from the gatepost and said 'purr' to her and rubbed round and round her legs. Then Mrs Lock stood up very straight and looked over the gate at my little sister.

Mrs Lock said: 'Thank you for the card.'

All the time the smoky-coloured cat was purring and rubbing, rubbing and purring round and round my sister's legs and Mrs Lock said: 'My cat likes you. His name is Tibbles. Stroke him.'

And my sister did stroke him, and after that she stroked him every time she went past Mrs Lock's gate and found him sitting there in the sunshine. And although Mrs Lock often saw her stroking him she never said 'Don't you meddle with my cat' to her.

AND when Christmas time came Mrs Lock sent my sister a card with robins and holly and shiny glittery stuff on it that was even more lovely than the pussy-cat card.

What a Jealous Child!

WHEN my sister was a naughty little girl she had a godmother-auntie whom she loved very much.

This godmother-auntie was a very, very kind, and very, very pretty young lady. My little sister used to say that she was like a fairy in a book. She had curly gold hair and twinkling blue eyes and she was always laughing and singing.

And she was never cross. She used to have a lovely hat with cherries on it, and one day my greedy sister pulled the cherries off her hat and tried to eat them, and she didn't grumble at all. When she saw the dreadful face my naughty little sister was making when she found that those hat-cherries were full of nasty cotton-wool stuff she only laughed, and said: 'If you'd *told* me you wanted them to play with you could have had them, and then I would have explained that they were not real.'

And when our mother scolded my sister this pretty lady said: 'Don't worry, I was going to put a rose on that hat anyway.'

And the next time she came to see us she *had* put a rose on her hat – a big pink one, and to please my little sister she had brought along a small pink rose for her to wear on *her* hat! 'Only don't try to eat that,' she said, 'because it is made of silk and won't taste at all nice.'

Wasn't she kind?

This beautiful godmother worked in a big sweetie shop in London where they made specially grand sweeties in a big kitchen behind the shop, and she used to tell my sister and me all about how the sweeties were made.

She told us how the sweeties were rolled in sugar and cut with real silver knives and how all the fruity pieces in them came right across the sea from France in wooden boxes, and we were very interested.

She always brought us a big box of sweeties from her

shop and they were grander than any sweeties we'd ever seen before. They were in a very smart silky box with flowers on it, and the box was tied up with real hair-ribbony ribbon that our mother always put away in her ribbon box.

When our mother saw the beautiful tied-up box she always said: 'It looks too pretty to open.' But we *did* open it.

And when the box was opened she would say: 'They

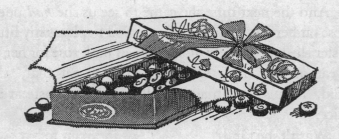

look too nice to eat.' But we *did* eat them, and Mother always had the first one – and she always took the almondy one in the middle with the green bits sticking out of it, because there was only one of those, and she didn't want my sister and me to be cross about who should have it.

My little sister loved those boxes of sweeties because her godmother-aunt had told her all about the big shop and the place where they were made, and she would be very careful before she chose her sweet, and when she did choose it she would say: 'Tell me about this one, godma-aunt.'

And she would hear all over again about silver knives and French cherries and men in white caps who twisted the sweetie stuff on hooks and pulled it out and p-u-l-l-e-d it out to make it clear and shiny.

When her beautiful godmother said: 'Pulled it out' she would make pulling out faces and speak in a pulling out voice; she would say: 'P-u-l-l-e-d i-t o-u-t' – like that.

How my sister would laugh. She always wanted to hear about the pulling out of the sweetie stuff when her godmother came to see us.

We were always glad to see my little sister's godmother, she was so very nice. My little sister liked seeing her best of all. She liked to climb on to her godmother's lap and stare at her pretty smily face. She would pat her cheeks and say: 'Sing to me, godma-aunt. Sing me a funny song.'

And her godmother would sing her all sorts of funny songs until my sister's eyes got all peepy and teary with laughing so much.

Then my sister, who was not a kissing child at all, would hug and kiss her pretty godmother-auntie and say: 'I do love you, you nice lady!'

Wasn't she a lovely godmother to have?

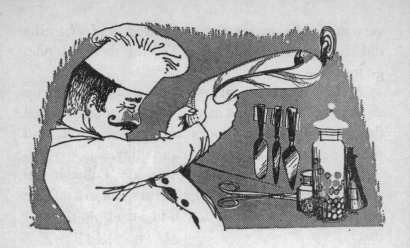

Now, you wouldn't think that anyone could ever be cross with such a dear lady, would you?

You would be surprised to hear that someone shouted at her and said: 'Go away, I don't want you,' wouldn't you?

I know I was surprised when my sister behaved like that to her dear godmother. But she did. And do you know why? It's because she was an unpleasant, jealous girl.

You see, one day her dear godmother brought a great tall man to see us. She had never brought anyone else before, and my sister didn't quite like it. She liked to have her godmother on her own. She said: 'I'm shy,' and ran and hid her face in Mother's lap, and when Mother told her to sit on a chair and to stop being silly, she sat and stared at her godmother-aunt and the great tall man and looked cross as cross.

Do you know why she behaved like that?

It was because the great tall man liked her godmother-aunt too and it was because her godmother-aunt liked the tall man very much.

My naughty little sister didn't want her godmother to like anyone but her, and she didn't want the big tall man to like her godmother.

She was jealous. And that is a very nasty thing to be, isn't it. What a good thing you aren't a child like that.

My sister pretended that she didn't want any sweeties, and her poor godmother looked quite worried.

'But Albert made some of them,' she said.

Albert was the great tall man.

Our godmother started to tell us all about Albert making the sweeties, but my sister wouldn't listen. She got down from her chair and said: 'I want to go to bed now.'

Do you know that was in the morning, and she hadn't had her dinner. Wasn't she being awkward?

Mother said: 'You behave yourself, you naughty little girl.'

But the beautiful godmother-auntie said: 'Don't be cross with her, I think she's not sure about Albert.'

She smiled very kindly at my sister and said: 'You must like Albert, duckie. Albert and I are going to get married very soon and we shall be living in a dear little house and you can come and stay with us.' And she came over to my sister in a kind way.

When my sister heard this, when she heard that the great tall man and her pretty godmother-aunt were going to be married, she was so cross that she said what I told you.

She said: 'GO AWAY. I DON'T WANT YOU.'

She said: 'I don't want you and I don't want that great tall man. You can go away now.'

Oh dear! Our mother was cross! But what do you think? That great big tall Albert man started to laugh, and he had such a loud roary laugh that my sister forgot to be jealous and stared at him.

When Albert laughed my sister's godmother began to laugh too, and they made so much noise that our mother began to laugh as well, and so did I – you never heard so much laughing.

Then that funny Albert man got up and opened a big bag that he had brought with him, and he took out a big, wide saucepan. Then he took out a bag of sugar and some butter and some treacle stuff in a tin. He was laughing all the time he did it because my sister was staring so much!

He took these things out to our mother's kitchen and he began to cook all the sugar and stuff in his saucepan. He didn't say anything, he just cooked.

No one had ever done a thing like that in our house before, so my sister went on being not jealous, and went out into the kitchen to see what he was doing instead.

When Albert saw my sister looking at him he put his hand into his bag and took out a white hat and *put it on his head*.

And he cooked and cooked and stirred with a spoon and cooked until all the sugar-butter-treacly stuff began to smell very nice indeed.

Then Albert took the saucepan off the stove, and did another funny thing.

He took the towel off the hook behind our kitchen door, and he wiped the hook very clean with our mother's dish-cloth and dried it beautifully on the tea towel.

My sister's eyes said 'O' 'O', she was so astonished.

Then, all of a sudden, Albert took the warm sticky stuff out of the saucepan and threw it over the hook.

73

Then he got a hold on the end of it and he p-u-l-l-e-d it and he p-u-l-l-e-d it. Then he twisted it up and he threw it back over the hook and he p-u-l-l-e-d and p-u-l-l-e-d it again, quick as quick.

It was just like my sister's godmother had told us. And it wasn't in the shop-kitchen either, it was in our own mother's own kitchen.

Albert pulled that stuff until it was clear and then he took it off the hook, quick as quick! It was all long and twisty.

It was a beautiful thing to do, wasn't it?

Albert didn't speak to my sister, he just spoke out loud to himself; he said: 'I wonder if it tastes all right?'

He got a hammer and began to break the long twisty piece of toffee-stuff. When he did this, a piece jumped right off the table and fell by my sister's foot.

Our kitchen smelled so nice and the sweetie looked so nice, that my sister picked that piece up and popped it into her mouth and it was *quite delicious*.

Now she wasn't jealous at all. She was proud. She was proud to think that she knew such a clever man. 'It is very, very nice, Albert,' she said. 'You are very clever.'

Then she laughed and Albert laughed, and Albert let her put his funny white cap on, and her godmother lifted her up so that she could see herself in the glass wearing the white cap, and everyone was very happy.

My sister looked at her lovely smiling godmother and the great, tall, clever Albert and she said: 'I don't mind Albert being my godmother-uncle after all.'

The Smart Girl

ONE day, when I was a little girl and my little sister was sometimes naughty, the Mayor of our town invited us to a children's garden party. Bad Harry was invited too, and so were all the other children who lived near us.

When Mrs Cocoa heard that my little sister was going to the Mayor's party she was very pleased because she loved my bad little sister very much, and so she made her a beautiful party dress to wear.

Mrs Cocoa said that she had some nice material called Indian muslin in her drawer that would be just the thing for a party-dress.

The Indian muslin was all white with little white needlework flowers all over it. Mrs Cocoa made it into a dress for my little sister, and when it was finished she put a pink ribbon round the middle of it, and pink bows on the sleeves, and she made a frilly petticoat to go underneath it; and when my little sister tried it on she looked just like a beautiful new doll straight out of the box.

Bad Harry was there when my sister tried her dress on and he opened his eyes very wide.

'Nice,' said Bad Harry. 'You *do* look nice.'

And he said 'Nice and nice and nice' to show my sister how very smart he thought she looked.

My little sister didn't say anything. She just stood on the table and looked at herself in the mirror over the mantelpiece and was so very pleased she couldn't talk at all.

She was quite quiet until dear Mrs Cocoa said: 'Don't you like it?' Then she spoke. She said: 'Oh, Mrs Cocoa, I am just like a fairy. I think I must take it off quickly before it gets dirty.'

That was a surprising thing for my little sister to say, for as a rule she didn't mind being dirty a bit.

When our mother had taken the dress off for her, my funny sister ran to Mrs Cocoa and hugged her and kissed her and said: 'Dear Mrs Cocoa, I love my smart dress. I love it very much. *I love me in it, too.*'

She wouldn't hug Mrs Cocoa while she had the dress on, because she was afraid of spoiling it. Wasn't she funny?

Before the party day my little sister often went upstairs and asked our mother to let her peep into the wardrobe and see the Indian muslin dress, but she didn't want to try it on again, she wouldn't even touch it. She said she wanted it to be absolutely beautiful for the party. Wasn't she a strange child?

When the party day came, and she saw me getting

ready to go, my little sister said : 'Mother, I will wear my smart dress *now*.' And she stood straight and good on a chair while Mother washed her, and straight and good when she was dressed, AND straight and good when her hair was brushed, because she wanted to look just like a fairy.

Bad Harry came to call for us. 'Come on, come on,' he said, because he was impatient, but my little sister would not hurry. She said 'Good-bye' to our mother in a very quiet voice, and she took my hand like a good girl and walked along very neatly in her white shoes, not scuffling the dust or anything!

Mrs Cocoa came to her gate to see us off and my sister waved her hand to her. 'I can't kiss you, Mrs Cocoa,' she said, 'because I am all neat and nice,' and although Bad Harry said 'Hurry! Hurry!' and ran ahead and back again and again she still walked very nicely and slowly with me.

At last we came to the Mayor's Garden Party place. It did look grand! The Mayor had hung lots of little coloured flags all round his garden, and the big gates were open and a band was playing, and we could hear Punch-and-Judy noises and see stripy tents inside. Bad Harry was so excited that he just dashed ahead of us, and would have gone in on his own, if the gate man hadn't asked him for his invitation card that I was carrying for him!

There were a lot of people crowding round the gate watching the children going to the party, and one lady said: 'Oh, the little duckie,' when she saw my neat and nice sister, and my little sister felt very proud. But she didn't turn her head, and she didn't let go of my hand, because she wanted to look as fairy-like as possible!

The Mayor had made a lovely party for us. We soon found that the stripy tents had all sorts of interesting things in them. Things that you could do without paying for them. It was just like a lovely *free* fair!

There were hoop-la's and magic fish-ponds and swings and pony-rides and Mr Punch and a conjuror, all as free as free. There was even a coconut shy, and we saw some of the bigger children throwing balls at the coconuts.

Wasn't it kind of the Mayor? We saw him walking in the garden with a gold chain round his neck, and he smiled at us and asked if we were having a good time. We said: 'Yes, thank you,' and he said: 'Good. Good.'

And we were enjoying ourselves. At least I was. And Bad Harry was. But my little sister didn't seem to be enjoying it very much at all. You see, she was afraid of spoiling her smart dress, and when the gentlemen with the roundabouts said: 'Come on now, who wants a ride?' she couldn't say 'Me! me!' because she wanted to look smart and she was afraid she might get her dress dirty on the roundabouts; and when the fish-pond young lady said: 'Come and fish for a magic prize,' she said: 'No, thank you, I might get wet!'

Bad Harry fished and he won a tin whistle, but,

although she wanted a tin whistle very much, she wouldn't fish, oh no!

When we went to see Mr Punch she stood at the back of the crowd because of her sticking out dress, and she was so far away that when Mr Punch smacked his baby, she didn't hear the nice man by the Punch show saying: 'It's all right, children, he isn't really hurting it, you know!' and so of course she cried, and then she had to stop crying because she might make her Indian muslin dress all teary.

Bad Harry got quite cross at last and he said: 'Why did you wear that silly old dress?'

My sister said: 'It's not silly. It's smart.'

And Harry said: 'It's smart *and* it's silly if you can't do anything in it.'

My little sister said: 'I want to be smart.'

Then Bad Harry said: 'Well, if you keep on being smart like that you won't be able to have any of the Mayor's nice tea that the ladies are putting on the tables in that big tent over there. It's a very nice tea,' Bad Harry said. 'There are lots of cakes and jellies. I know because I've just been over there to look.'

When my little sister heard about the tea and the jellies and when she thought about the roundabouts and the fish-pond she began to feel quite sorry. But she didn't want to spoil her smart dress.

She thought and thought. She saw the other children running about and sliding on slides and eating ice-cream and throwing balls at coconuts, and then she had a funny idea.

Very, very quietly she walked away from the fair-place and round behind some bushes where no one could see her. I didn't notice her go, because Bad Harry and I were trying to throw rings over some hooks on the hoop-la stall.

When I *did* find that she had gone, I was very worried, especially as a big gentleman in a red coat began to bang on a tray and call out: 'Now, children, line up, and we will go in to tea.'

I must say I didn't want to go and look for my sister just at tea-time. I thought that the other children might eat all the cakes and jellies and things before I found her, and I wouldn't like that much.

But I *had* promised to look after her, so I began to ask people if they had seen her.

I was just asking a lady, when I heard everyone burst out laughing.

All the boys and girls laughed, and the roundabout man, and the Punch man and the fish-pond lady, and the Mayor and Bad Harry. They laughed and laughed and laughed.

They were laughing at my naughty little sister!

What do you think she had done?

She had got so tired of being careful of her beautiful dress that she had gone behind the bushes and *taken it off*. I don't know how she managed on her own – but she did.

She had taken off her dress and her lovely frilly petticoat and had put them very carefully over a garden seat, and out she jumped, her old noisy jumping self again, skipping up and down in her little white vest and her little white knickers! And she was laughing too.

'*Now* I can have swings, and fish-ponds, and roundabouts and a *big tea*,' she shouted. 'Now I can be M E again.'

She was very pleased with her good idea.

'I shan't spoil my beautiful dress now,' she said. 'Aren't I a clever girl?'

What would you have said if she had been your Naughty Little Sister?

My Naughty Little Sister
is a Curly Girl

THERE was a little girl called Winnie who used to come and see us sometimes when I was a little girl with a naughty little sister.

This girl Winnie was a very quiet, tidy child. She never rushed about and shouted or played dirty games, and she always wore neat clean dresses.

Winnie had some of those long round and round curls like chimney-pots that hung round her head in a very tidy way, and when Winnie moved her head these little curls jumped up and down. Mother told us that these curls were called *ringlets*.

One day, when Winnie and her mother were spending the afternoon at our house, my sister sat staring very hard at Winnie's ringlets, and all of a sudden she got up and went over to her and pushed one of her little fingers into one of Winnie's tidy ringlets.

Then, because the ringlet looked so nice on her finger, she pushed another finger into another ringlet.

Now, if anyone had interfered with *my sister's hair* she would have screamed and screamed – she even made a fuss when our mother brushed it – but Winnie sat still and quiet in a very mousy way, although I don't think she liked having her hair meddled with any more than my sister would have done.

Winnie's mother certainly didn't like it, and she said in a polite firm voice: 'Please don't fiddle with Winifred's hair, dear, the curls may come out.'

Then Winnie's mother said to our mother: 'They take such ages to put in every night.'

When Winnie's mother said this, my funny sister thought that the curls would come right out of Winnie's head if she touched them too much. And she thought that Winnie's mother would have to pick all the curls up and put them back into Winnie's head at night-time. So she stopped touching Winnie's hair at once, and went and sat down again.

She didn't think she would like to be Winnie with falling-out curls.

My little sister sat looking at Winnie though, in case a curl should fall out on its own, but when it didn't, she got tired of looking at her, and went out into the garden instead to talk over the fence to dear Mrs Cocoa Jones.

'Mrs Cocoa,' she said, 'Winnie has funny curls.'

Mrs Cocoa was surprised when my sister said this, so she told her what Winnie's mother had said about the curls coming out.

Now, Mrs Cocoa was a kind polite lady and she didn't laugh at my sister for making such a funny mistake. She just told her all about how Winnie's mother made Winnie's curls for her.

Mrs Cocoa told my sister how, when *she* was a little girl, her kind old grandmother had curled *her* hair. She said that her grandmother had made her hair damp with a wet brush and had twisted her hair up in little pieces of rag, and how she had gone to bed with her hair twisted up like this and how, next morning, when her grandmother had undone her curlers she had had ringlets just like Winnie's.

My sister was very interested to hear all this.

'Of course,' Mrs Cocoa said, 'my granny only did up

my hair on Saturday nights so that it would be curly for Sunday. On ordinary week-nights I had two little pig-tails like yours.'

When my sister heard Mrs Cocoa saying about how her grandmother curled her hair for her, she began to smile as big as that.

'I know, Mrs Cocoa,' she said, 'you can make me a curly girl.'

Mrs Cocoa said that my sister would have to sit still and not scream then, and my sister said she would be very still indeed, so Mrs Cocoa said : 'Well then, if your mother is willing, I'll pop in tonight and put some curlers in for you.'

After that, my sister went back into the house, and sat very quietly looking at Winnie and Winnie's beauti-ful ringlets and smiling in a pussy-cat pleased way to herself.

She didn't say anything to Winnie and her mother about what kind Mrs Cocoa was going to do, but when they had gone she told Mother and me all about it, and Mother said it was very kind of Mrs Cocoa to offer to make ringlets of my sister's hair, and she said : 'Mrs Cocoa can try anyway, although I can't think *how* you will sit still without making a fuss.'

But my sister said : 'I want ringlets like Winnie's,' and she said it in a very loud voice to show that she wouldn't fuss, so our mother didn't say anything else,

and when Mrs Cocoa came over at my sister's bedtime, with a lot of strips of pink rag, and asked for my sister's hairbrush and a basin of water, our mother fetched them for her without saying a word about how my sister usually fussed.

Now, my sister had said that she wasn't going to be a naughty girl when Mrs Cocoa curled her hair, and she knew that Mother expected her to be naughty, and that I expected her to be naughty, so, although she found that she didn't like having her hair twisted up into rags very much, *she was good as gold*.

My sister didn't like having her hair twisted up into those rags one bit. You see, her hair was rather long, and Mrs Cocoa had to twist *and* twist *very tightly indeed* to make sure that the curlers would stay in; and the tighter the curl-rags were the more uncomfortable they felt.

But my sister didn't say so. She sat very good and quiet and she thought about all those lovely Winnie-ringlets, and when Mrs Cocoa had finished she thanked her very nicely indeed and went upstairs with Rosy-Primrose, with her hair all curled up tight with little pink rags sticking up all over her head.

But, oh dear.

Have *you* ever tried to sleep with curlers in *your* hair? My sister tried and tried, but wherever she turned her head there was a little knob of hair to lie on and it was most uncomfortable.

She tried to go to sleep with her nose in the pillow but that was most feathery and unpleasant.

In the end the poor child went to sleep with her head right over the edge of the bed and her arm tight round the bedpost to keep herself from falling out.

That wasn't comfortable either, so she woke up.

When my little sister woke up she shouted because

she couldn't remember why she was lying in such a funny way, and our mother had to come in to her.

When Mother saw how hard it was for my little sister to sleep with her curlers in, she said perhaps they had better come out, and that made my naughty little sister cry because she did want Winnie-ringlets, until Mother said: 'Well, if you want curls don't fuss then,' and went back to her own bed.

After that my poor sister slept and woke up and slept and woke up all night, but she didn't shout any more, and when morning came she was sleepy and cross and peepy-eyed.

But when she had had her breakfast, Mrs Cocoa came in to undo the curlers, and my sister cheered up and began to smile.

She sat very still while kind Mrs Cocoa took out the

rags and carefully combed each ringlet into shape, and when Mrs Cocoa had finished, and my sister climbed up to see herself in the mirror she smiled like anything.

And I smiled and Mother smiled.

She was a curly girl – curlier than Winnie even, because she had a lot more hair than Winnie had. She had real ringlets that you could push your fingers into!

My sister was a proud girl that day, she sat about in a still quiet way – just like Winnie did, and after dinner she fell fast asleep in her chair.

When my sister woke up she sat for a little while and did a lot of thinking, then she got down from her chair and went round to see Mrs Cocoa.

'Thank you very much, Mrs Cocoa, for making me a curly girl,' my sister said, 'but I don't think I will be curly any more. It makes me too sleepy to be curly.'

'I know why Winnie is so quiet now,' my sister said, 'it's because she can't sleep for curlers. I think I would rather be me, fast asleep with pigtails.'

And Mrs Cocoa said: 'That's a very good idea, I think. Anyway who wants *you* to look like that Winnie?'

Some Other Young Puffins

LUCKY DIP *Ruth Ainsworth*
ANOTHER LUCKY DIP

Stories from the BBC's *Listen With Mother*. Seven of the ever-popular *Charles* stories are included.

THE TEN TALES OF SHELLOVER *Ruth Ainsworth*

The Black Hens, the Dog and the Cat didn't like Shellover the tortoise at first, until they discovered what wonderful stories he told.

MY FIRST BIG STORY BOOK ed. *Richard Bamberger*
MY SECOND BIG STORY BOOK
MY THIRD BIG STORY BOOK

A wonderful hoard of nursery and bed-time stories ranging from traditional English favourites to strange new tales from other lands.

LITTLE PETE STORIES *Leila Berg*

More favourites from *Listen With Mother*, about a small boy who plays mostly by himself. Illustrated by Peggy Fortnum.

THE CASTLE OF YEW *Lucy M. Boston*

Joseph visits the magic garden where the yew trees are shaped like castles – and finds himself shrunk small enough to crawl inside one.

THE HAPPY ORPHELINE *Natalie Savage Carlson*
A BROTHER FOR THE ORPHELINES

The 20 little orphaned girls who live with Madame Flattot are terrified of being adopted beause they are so happy.

FIVE DOLLS IN A HOUSE *Helen Clare*

A little girl called Elizabeth finds a way of making herself small and visits her dolls in their own house.

TELL ME A STORY   *Eileen Colwell*

TELL ME ANOTHER STORY

TIME FOR A STORY

Stories, verses, and finger plays for children of 3 to 6, collected by the greatest living expert on the art of children's story-telling.

MY NAUGHTY LITTLE SISTER   *Dorothy Edwards*

WHEN MY NAUGHTY LITTLE SISTER WAS GOOD

MY NAUGHTY LITTLE SISTER AND BAD HARRY

These famous stories were originally by a mother to her own children. Ideal for reading aloud. For ages 4 to 8.

MISS HAPPINESS AND MISS FLOWER   *Rumer Godden*

Nona was lonely far away from her home in India, and the two dainty Japanese dolls, Miss Happiness and Miss Flower, were lonely too. But once Nona started building them a proper Japanese house they all felt happier. Illustrated by Jean Primrose.

HERE COMES THURSDAY   *Michael Bond*

THURSDAY AHOY!

THURSDAY RIDES AGAIN

THURSDAY IN PARIS

The mouse arrived on Thursday, so that's what the Pecks named him when they adopted him into their family of church mice.

THIS LITTLE PUFFIN ...   *Elizabeth Matterson*

An enchanting collection of musical games, action songs and finger plays, which no mother or nursery school can afford to be without (*Young Puffin Original*).

MEET MARY KATE   *Helen Morgan*

Charmingly told stories of a 4-year-old's everyday life in the country. Illustrated by Shirley Hughes.

ROM-BOM-BOM AND OTHER STORIES   *Antonia Ridge*

A collection of animal stories written by the distinguished children's author and broadcaster. For 4- to 8-year-olds.

PUFFIN BOOK OF NURSERY RHYMES *Peter and Iona Opie*

The first comprehensive collection of nursery rhymes to be produced as a paperback, prepared for Puffins by the leading authorities on children's lore. 220 pages, exquisitely illustrated on every page by Pauline Baynes. (*A Young Puffin Original.*)

LITTLE OLD MRS PEPPERPOT *Alf Prøysen*
MRS PEPPERPOT TO THE RESCUE
MRS PEPPERPOT IN THE MAGIC WOOD
MRS PEPPERPOT'S OUTING

Gay little stories about an old woman who suddenly shrinks to the size of a pepperpot.

DEAR TEDDY ROBINSON *Joan G. Robinson*
ABOUT TEDDY ROBINSON
TEDDY ROBINSON HIMSELF
KEEPING UP WITH TEDDY ROBINSON

Teddy Robinson was Deborah's teddy bear and such a very nice, friendly, cuddly bear that he went everywhere with her and had even more adventures than she did.

THE ADVENTURES OF GALLDORA *Modwena Sedgwick*
NEW ADVENTURES OF GALLDORA

This lovable rag doll belonged to Marybell, who wasn't always very careful to look after her, so Galldora was always getting lost – in a field with a scarecrow, on top of a roof, and in all sorts of other strange places.

SOMETHING TO DO *Septima*

Suggestions for games to play and things to make and do each month, from January to December. It is designed to help mothers with young children at home. (*A Young Puffin Original.*)

PONDER AND WILLIAM *Barbara Softly*
PONDER AND WILLIAM ON HOLIDAY
PONDER AND WILLIAM AT HOME

Ponder the panda looks after William's pyjamas and is a wonderful companion in these all the year round adventures. Illustrated by Diana John. (*Young Puffin Originals.*)

CLEVER POLLY AND THE STUPID WOLF *Catherine Storr*
POLLY AND THE WOLF AGAIN

Clever Polly manages to think of lots of good ideas to stop the stupid wolf from eating her.

ROBIN *Catherine Storr*

Robin discovers the shell called 'The Freedom of the Seas' – and soon he's the wonder of his family.

DANNY FOX *David Thomson*

Clever Danny Fox helps the Princess to marry the fisherman she loves and comes safely home to his hungry family. (*A Young Puffin Original.*)

DANNY FOX MEETS A STRANGER *David Thomson*

The stranger was a big grey wolf, and he was out to steal Danny's den and hunting grounds. (*A Young Puffin Original.*)

THE URCHIN *Edith Unnerstad*

The Urchin is only five years old – but already he has the Larsson family at sixes and sevens with his ingenious tricks and adventures.

LITTLE O *Edith Unnerstad*

The enchanting story of the youngest of the Pip Larsson family.

MAGIC IN MY POCKET *Alison Uttley*

A selection of short stories by this well-loved author, especially good for 5- and 6-year-olds.

LITTLE RED FOX *Alison Uttley*
MORE LITTLE RED FOX STORIES

Little Red Fox is adopted by kind Mr and Mrs Badger, but finds it hard to be as good as their own children.

THE PENNY PONY *Barbara Willard*

Life is never quite the same for Cathy and Roger after they find the penny pony in Mrs Boddy's shop. A delightful story for readers of 6 to 8.

GOBBOLINO THE WITCH'S CAT *Ursula Moray Williams*

Gobbolino's mother was ashamed of him because his eyes were blue instead of green, and he wanted to be loved instead of learning spells. So he goes in search of a friendly kitchen. Illustrated by the author.

ADVENTURES OF THE LITTLE WOODEN HORSE
Ursula Moray Williams

To help his master, a brave little horse sets out to sell himself and brings home a great fortune.